W9-ATS-581

Pease Public Library
1 Russell Street
Plymouth, NH 03264

When I Feel Sad

WRITTEN BY
Cornelia Maude Spelman

ILLUSTRATED BY
Kathy Parkinson

www.av2books.com

Your AV^2 Media Enhanced book gives you a fiction readalong online. Log on to www.av2books.com and enter the unique book code from this page to use your readalong.

Go to **www.av2books.com**, and enter this book's unique code.

BOOK CODE

J372234

AV^2 by Weigl brings you media enhanced books that support active learning.

AV^2 Readalong Navigation

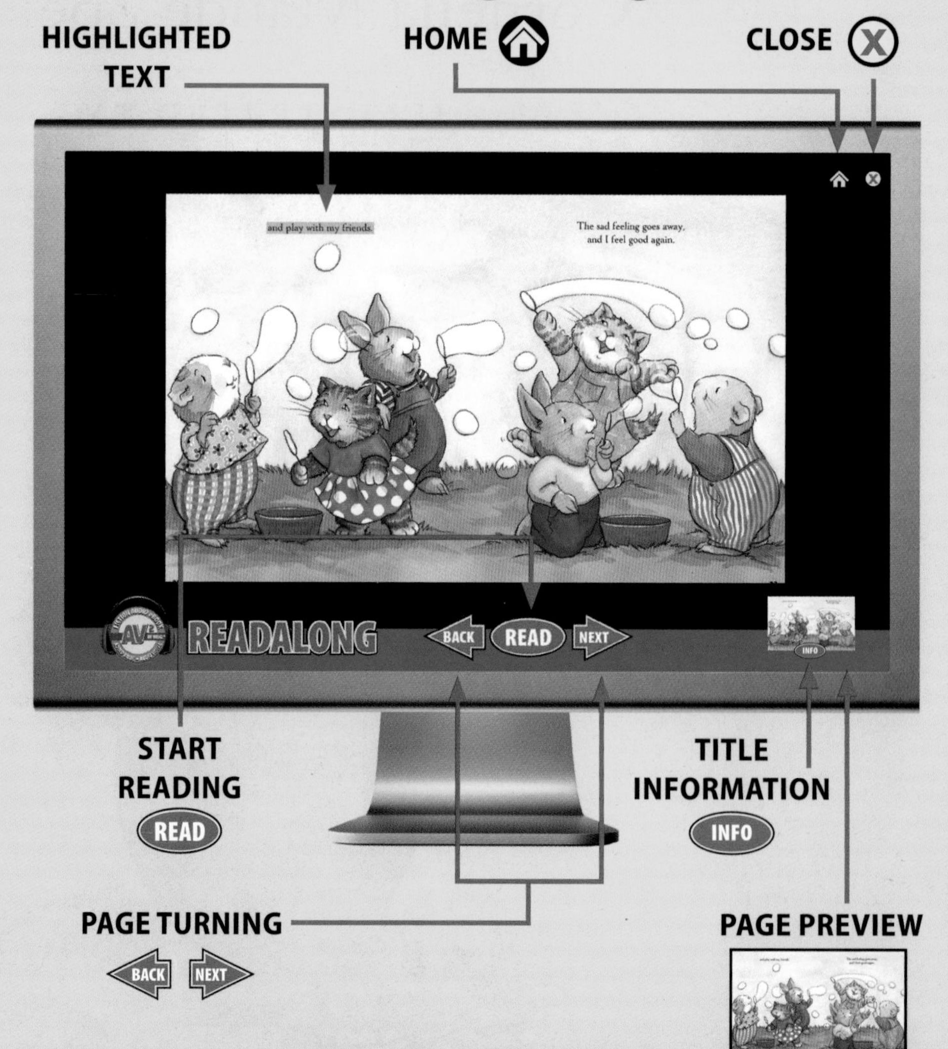

First Published by

Published by AV^2 by Weigl
350 5th Avenue, 59th Floor New York, NY 10118
Website: www.av2books.com www.weigl.com

Copyright ©2014 AV^2 by Weigl
All rights reserved. No part of this publication may be reproduced, stored in a retrieval system, or transmitted in any form or by any means, electronic, mechanical, photocopying, recording, or otherwise, without the prior written permission of the publisher.

Printed in the United States of America in North Mankato, Minnesota
1 2 3 4 5 6 7 8 9 0 17 16 15 14 13

052013
WEP250413

Library of Congress Control Number: 2013940831

ISBN 978-1-62127-908-2 (hardcover)
ISBN 978-1-48961-493-3 (single-user eBook)
ISBN 978-1-48961-494-0 (multi-user eBook)

Text copyright ©2002 by Cornelia Maude Spelman.
Illustrations copyright ©2002 by Kathy Parkinson.
Published in 2002 by Albert Whitman & Company.

Note to Parents and Teachers

It is painful for us when children are sad. Their sorrow makes us anxious to help them so that they can feel happy again. It also arouses our own feelings of sadness. Yet, if we didn't learn that it was okay to acknowledge and share our own unhappy feelings, we may deny or minimize our children's, or try to distract them from these feelings.

This reaction, while understandable, is not helpful. It teaches children not to pay attention to their feelings or share them with others. Children need to learn that sharing feelings with other human beings brings comfort. Some adults who did not learn this, who did not experience being understood and listened to, have problems in relationships. Others may turn for comfort to substances instead of to people.

But there is a difference between acknowledging a child's feeling, offering comfort, and overindulging. The child who is sad can be offered physical closeness, listening, and time to share his sadness, yet still be expected to pick up his toys, to carry on. It's a question of timing, of giving emotions their due before we offer activities which will help move the child past the sadness.

This book addresses ordinary sadness. We can help a child who grieves following a death or other major loss in these same ways, but we need to be attentive over a longer period of time. And when for too long a child stays sad, cries frequently, is listless, has problems eating and sleeping—seek professional help. Even very young children can suffer from clinical depression, which requires intervention.

We want our children to know that we value all of their feelings—positive or negative; that all of us, children and adults, experience such feelings; and that we know how to deal with them. We want to build our children's confidence in their coping ability, so that they will be able to say, "When I feel sad, I know I won't stay sad."

Cornelia Maude Spelman, A.C.S.W., L.C.S.W.

Sometimes I feel sad.

I feel sad when someone won't let me play,

or when I really want to tell about
something and nobody listens.

When someone else is sad,
I feel sad, too.

I feel sad when I want to be with somebody,

but he's not there.

If something bad happens, I feel sad.

When I can't have something I really,
really want, or when I lose something special,
I feel sad.

When someone is cross with me, I feel sad,

and I feel sad when I get hurt.

Sad is a cloudy, tired feeling.
Nothing seems fun when I feel sad.

I don't like feeling sad!
I want sadness to go away.

But everyone feels sad sometimes.

When I feel sad, there are ways to feel better.
I can tell someone I'm sad.

"That's OK," they say, and sit close to me.
It feels good to be close to someone
when I'm sad.

It's all right to show I'm sad.
It's all right to cry.

After a while, I'm done crying. But I might still want to talk about what made me sad.

Pretty soon I start to feel better. I want to go to the park and swing on the swings.

I want to make something

and play with my friends.

The sad feeling goes away,
and I feel good again.

When I feel sad, I know I won't stay sad!